To Sarah, for helping me live my dream job

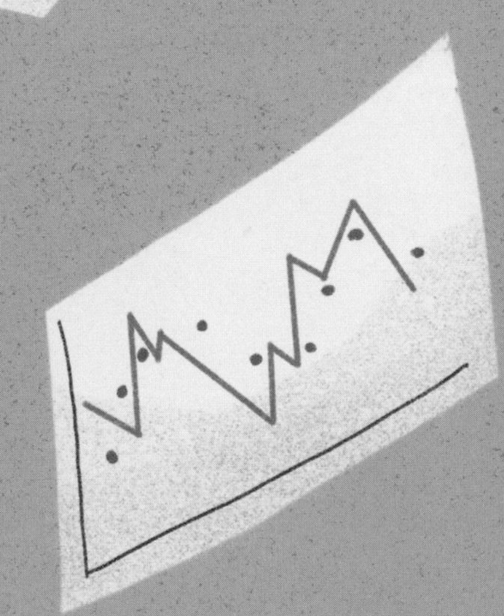

First U.S. edition 2018

Library of Congress Catalog Card Number pending
ISBN 978-0-7636-9896-6

18 19 20 21 22 23 TLF 10 9 8 7 6 5 4 3 2 1

Printed in Dongguan, Guangdong, China

This book was typeset in Gill Sans.
The illustrations were done in mixed media.

TEMPLAR BOOKS

an imprint of
Candlewick Press
99 Dover Street
Somerville, Massachusetts 02144
www.candlewick.com

DUCK GETS A JOB

Sonny Ross

templar books
an imprint of Candlewick Press

This is Duck.
Duck wanted a job.

All Duck's friends had jobs in the city,
and they never stopped talking about them.

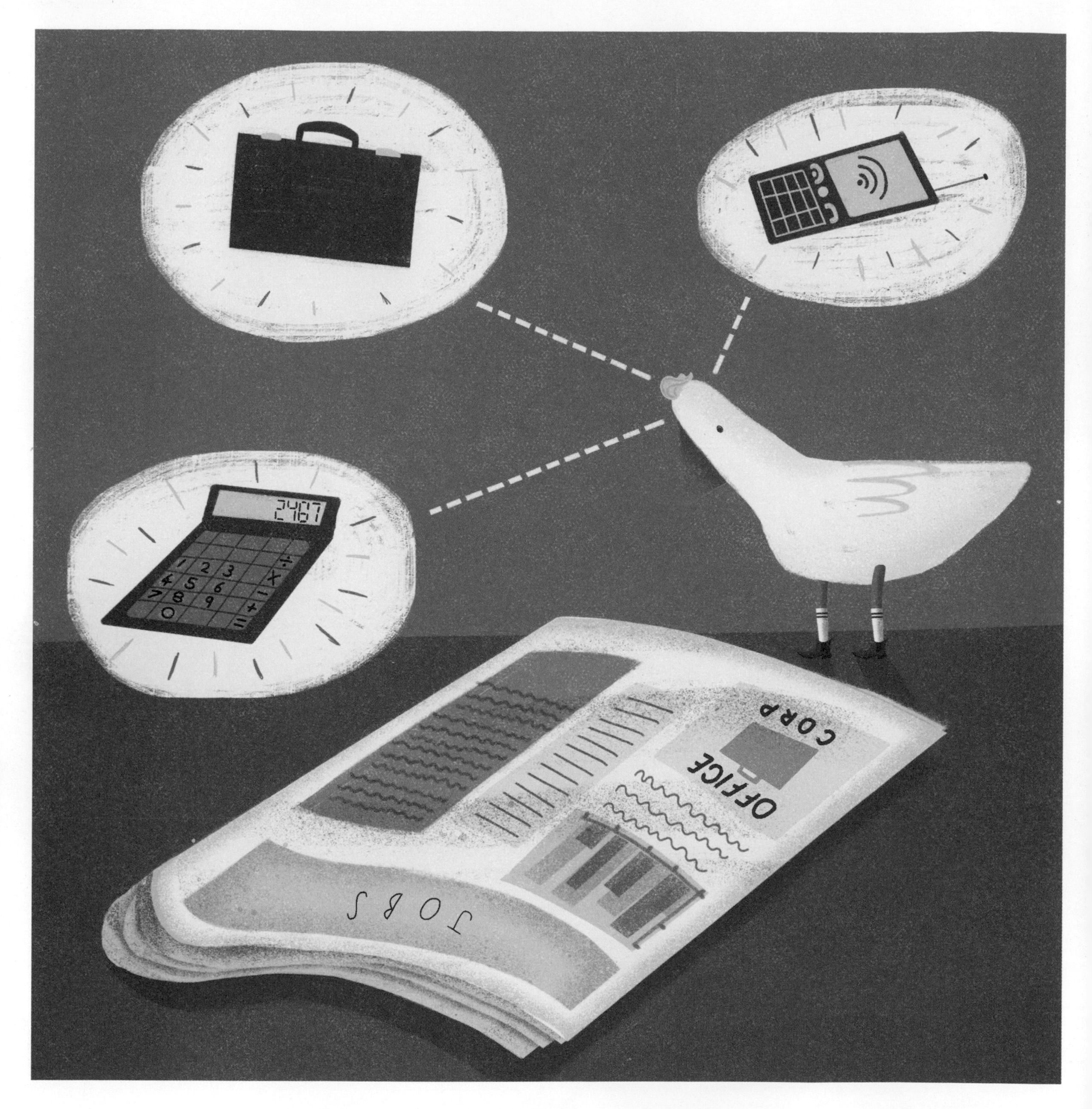

So Duck looked at the ads for city jobs.
They seemed boring, but he applied anyway.
And he got an interview!

He couldn't decide what to wear to the job interview.
He didn't want to make a bad first impression.
He opted for a professional look.

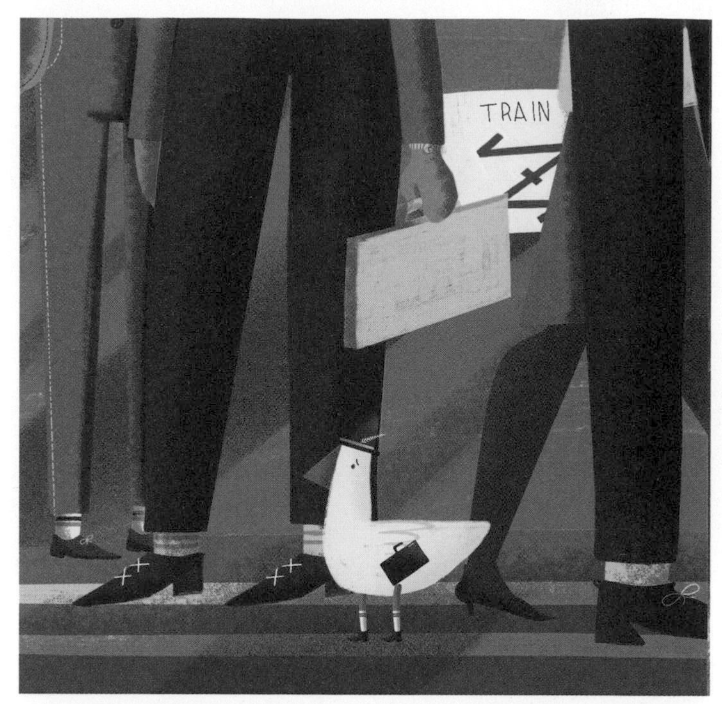

Next, Duck had to decide how to get there.
Flying would make him tired and sweaty, but
public transportation is tricky for ducks.

He chose to walk.

He got lost.

When Duck finally arrived in the city,
he had to get a taxi so he wouldn't be late.

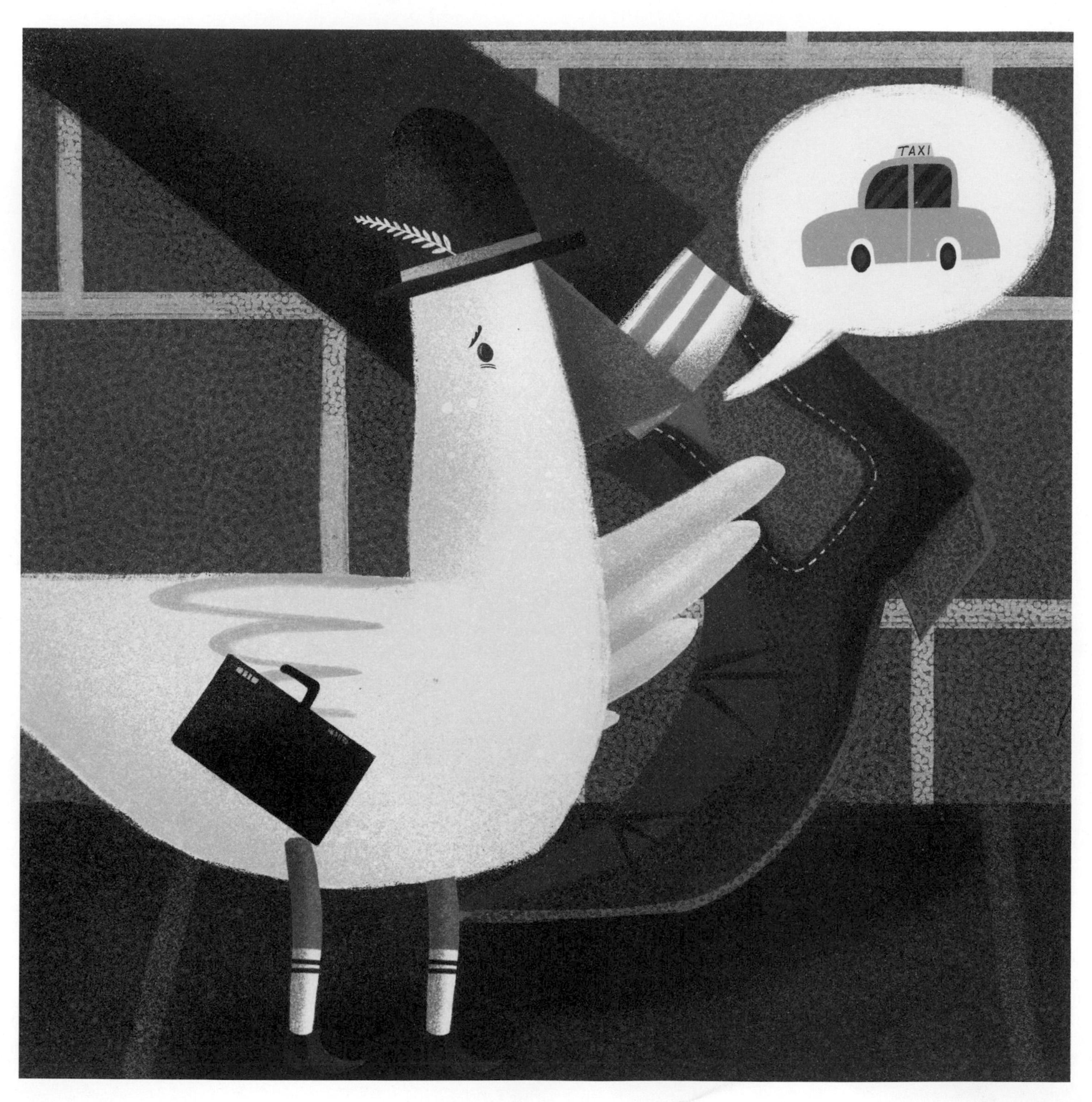

In the taxi, he gave himself a pep talk.

CALM DOWN
BE COOL
BE YOURSELF
PIE
RELAX
TAXI

In the interview, Duck wasn't cool,
professional, *or* relaxed. He was very nervous.

But he got the job!

Duck soon realized that spreadsheets full of facts
and figures did not interest him at all . . .

though he did have a nice nap.

OFFICE CORP

Before he left that night, Duck quit.

He had always wanted to be an artist.

So Duck found an ad for a job
that better suited his interests.

For his interview, he dressed in his natural look
and put samples of his best work in a portfolio.

He checked his route to make sure he didn't get lost, and
he left plenty of time so he wouldn't be late.

He showed his work and he wasn't nervous at all.
He felt confident because he was being himself.

Duck got the job!
He was very happy.

Duck loved his new job.
There were no spreadsheets!

DUCKS ARE RAD

DUCKS
ARE
RAD

Duck was happy that he had decided to follow his dreams.

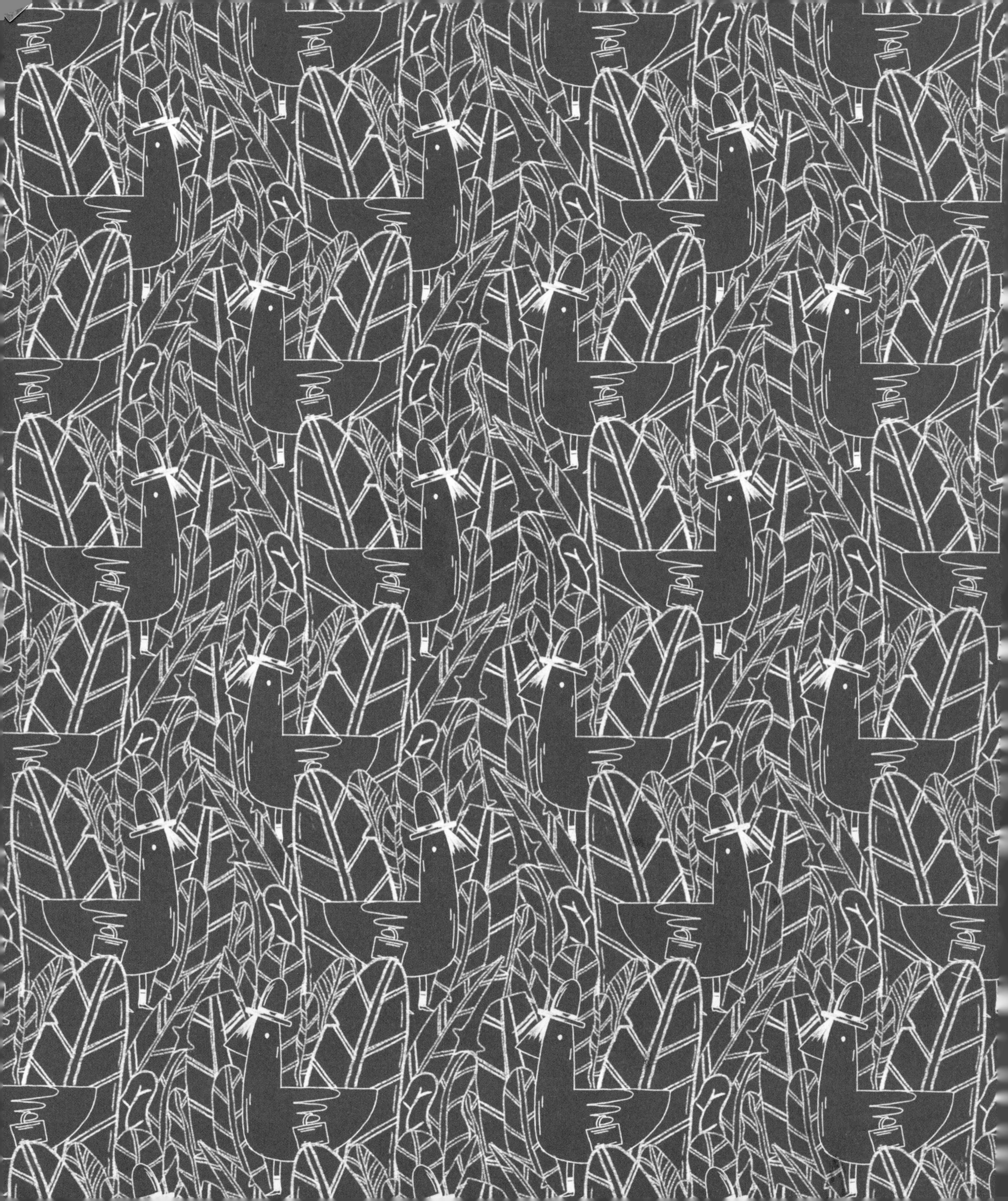